BodyPunk
Copyright © 2025 by their individual authors
Book & cover design by Ira Rat

This is a work of fiction. Names, characters, businesses, places, events, locales, and incidents are either the products of the author's imagination or used in a fictitious manner. Any resemblance to actual persons, living or dead, or actual events is purely coincidental.

This book may not be reproduced in whole or in part, except for the inclusion of brief quotations in a review, without permission in writing from the author or publisher. No part of this publication may be reproduced, stored in or introduced into retrieval system, or transmitted, in any form, or by any means (electronic, mechanical, photocopying, recording, or otherwise), without prior permission of the publisher.

Requests for permission should be directed to
filthylootpress@gmail.com

FIRST EDITION

BODYPUNK

And At Night, The Sirens
Joe Koch - 7

Nothing Here
Max Restaino - 29

Like Snowflakes Melting on Your Tongue
Xavier Garcia - 49

Split Dick David's First Post-Op Blowjob
Charlene Elsby - 64

Endless Wound
Sam Richard - 73

Filthy Loot
filthyloot.com

DO NOT FILE UNDER:
Extreme Horror

This book started at VoidCon when I found myself talking to an author I have admired for years about the differences between "extreme horror" and "splatterpunk."

Their answer was that all real Splatterpunk was *political*.

This decree landed well with me because I had already been making my own pronouncement to anyone who would listen to me (i.e. no one) that body horror is *philosophical*. The juxtaposition of these two ideas led to what you now hold in your hands.

The title of this introduction isn't an attempt to declare war or to disparage an entire genre, it's just a statement that these stories are not extreme horror. They might not even be splatterpunk or body horror either, who knows?.

Welcome to BodyPunk.

Jan, 20 2025, Ira Rat

And At Night, The Sirens
Joe Koch

It's already happened.

It's happening again.

Hot and clammy, her fingers clutch the cold white porcelain of the sink. Nerves on edge, giddy with sudden emptiness, with success, she leans into the pedestal. Eyes shut against the mirror's attack, she savors the luminous taste of bile. It reminds her of a knife gleaming in the sun.

The hard, smooth surface speaks to Synthia of permanence, of discipline, of something you can sterilize, unlike the filthy inside of the sink. The filthy insides of her body where food rots into shit-like clots of hair and slime clogging a drainpipe. Well, she won't let that happen, not tonight, not ever. She swears it. Not with the curses of her mother and all the mothers who came before damning her future. She spews the words of those witches out of her mouth, purging every bite.

Synthia's secret pride is that she's learned to gag at will with no finger, no implement. It's like a magic trick each time she heaves, a way to reverse her past mistakes.

Triumphant, she wants to be triumphant, except success is fleeting, and the lightning in her esophagus quickly sours. She needs to get back to the table—dinner must have cost him a fortune—needs to get her mouth rinsed and mascara blotted before someone walks in, especially some random adult. How she hates old ladies in restrooms nattering and touching. Any sign of weakness draws them hovering like flies to a corpse.

Inside of me there is a corpse, a skeleton waiting to be born.

She pulls at the fatty flesh around her face, eyes still closed, dizziness washing through her unstable membranes. Too soft, despite her vigilance. Too much padding over the bone. What should be gleaming white and impenetrable gives way at the slightest push. Below skin that should be porcelain but is not, there hides a meaty sack of tubes and bags and fluids sloshing and squelching and set to betray her at any instant with the bloated voice of her wrong form. Why couldn't she be like an insect with a hard carapace, armored for resistance? She can't let him see it, this fleshy mistake. Not with so much riding on their first date.

Come on, come on. Open your eyes.

In defiance, she turns on the faucet and tests the water before risking a look. The drain decides to be a mirror, to taunt her, its swirl a sickly reminder that she can't clean her pipes with caustic detergents. When the tempting sight of bright-colored plastic bottles with black and red warning labels leer at her with empty-eyed skulls, and the seductive pout of crossbones spark an overpowering urge, Synthia manages to resist. But what if she didn't? What if poison is an elixir, taken in the right dose?

Look up. He's waiting. Focus.

She stretches her jaw taut to make a smile, practicing her happy face, exposing her teeth. They ought to be whiter, but she can't do anything about that right now, not between dinner and dessert. She can't hose her drain-hole down and come out sparkling end to end. Best she can do is gargle and dab away the vague smear of drying tears.

When Synthia sweeps through the dining room, young and bright and chic, eyes can't avoid her. Jealous wives and men privileged or careless enough not to conceal their interest follow her, buoying her like waves, moving her through the room. Her very existence depends upon perception. She's sensitized to every nuance of approval or judgment. Directing her path through the maze of tables to avoid the garrulous group of young professionals, she slips lithely by the creepy middle-aged couple who are on their second bottle of Valpolicella, points her toes forward like her friend who took ballet taught her, and keeps her chin up, feigning confidence in the beauty she doesn't believe she has. Fairy brittle beneath her shimmering cloak of grace, she alights across from her date with practiced poise as the server serves a massive plate of chocolate cake.

The woman's long arms weave like a dancer placing forks, napkins, and plates between Synthia and her date. She's stately in a black button-down tucked into red cigarette pants, tall, dark-haired, with red high heels, black lacquered nails, and the speed born of expertise. Once she wishes them *bon appétit* and retreats, the boy leans forward and says, "I told them it was your birthday."

Rage tight enough to crack her teeth, Synthia sees how pleased he is with his little subterfuge, such a clever boy, *such a clever fucking boy*, but she keeps her face pinned and fitted, her smile stitched. "Oh, you shouldn't have." *You really, really shouldn't have cornered me like this.* "I couldn't eat another bite."

"Sure you can. You hardly had half your eggplant parm. Didn't you like it?"

Sincere like a puppy, he's a very nice boy, the type she needs to snag so she doesn't wind up an old hag, a virgin crone. God, she's terrified of sex, but she's got to do it soon. She's nearly twenty-two. The times she's tried, it just wouldn't go in, as if where other women open to pleasure, she's smooth and flat as a plastic Barbie doll. And wouldn't that be wonderful to be without pores and hairless, no garbage in or garbage out, a slick, hard, permanent surface of a girl instead of this messy endless process of shifting meat, always hungry or stinking or needing to be cleaned?

But never mind all that; quickly, she must negotiate with grace. "It was wonderful. No, I really pigged out. The servings here are huge." Giggling. Yes, and a little hair flip. That's it.

Her eyes catch the dark-haired server's. While it's normal for her to watch the table—it's her job—after all, there's something piercing and sticky in the woman's look. It scares Synthia like the sight of those big spiders that used to stalk her when she was up late alone, and her mom was out. She'd be doing a project or coloring at the kitchen table, and suddenly her skin would come alive, her heart would clutch between each beat. She'd feel eyes burning through her back, check the windows, but no one was there. Sit down again, and still know with every tingling follicle and awakened nerve that she was being watched, that she was prey.

The sensation grew worse the longer she tried to ignore it, even with her back to the wall, blinds drawn and safe, and she'd finally turned to look behind her once again, this time peering downward with a sense of inevitable dread. There, in the thin shadow of the baseboard, a black spider the size of a grown man's fist.

The server's gaze shifts. Synthia smiles at her date. Behind her vapid display she's excited and disturbed by the memory of the spider, by the fact that it's so specific, and yet she remembers nothing that happened after it spotted her. Or she spotted it. Did she do what a little girl would do, scream and run to her room? Did she crush it, black juice and pointed legs squirting under her shoe? Surely, she should remember something after the shock of recognition froze her in place. The empty memory tempts her. After the stark image of the spider, everything goes black.

"If you don't want any, do you dare me to put this whole piece of cake in my mouth? I bet I can eat the whole thing in one bite. Do you want to see me do it?"

He is grinning, pleased with himself as always, hands on the table as if he's going to pick up the plate and hoist the whole brown, moist, composted mass of sugar and fat to his mouth, spilling crumbs and smearing the frosting that's already the exact color and texture of a thick dark shit, making a spectacle of himself with goofy frat-boy bravado, sending Synthia into a panic to prevent him making her party to such public humiliation. She nearly yelps, "Why would you want to do that?"

"Because I can. You know those giant veggie burgers at Granger and Thyme's? I can put a whole burger in my mouth. This is nothing. I'll prove it."

Her eyes go a bit too wide. "Please don't."

He's smiling with ignorant delight, showing off a broad jawline and large healthy teeth, opening his mouth a little more as a taunt with each moment that she allows her demeanor to betray evidence of distress.

"I believe you!"

"No, you don't. Let me show you."

She recomposes her horror, tucks it away with her hidden rage, and lowers her voice. "Look, don't you dare hog all of my 'birthday' cake. If this is our first heist, we should enjoy the spoils together. Hand me a fork."

His grin softens into something less predatory. "You were really freaked out, weren't you? Why do you care so much about what other people think?"

"I don't like to draw attention to myself."

"Why not? You've got so much going for you. Might as well flaunt it." He lops off a thick slab of cake and offers it to her. "No? Okay. More for me, then."

He chews happily, takes another bite.

Synthia prods the edge of the cake with her fork, nipping off as little as she plausibly can.

Inside her chest, below the flesh too fleshy to be porcelain, beneath the ribcage and sternum of the skeleton yearning to escape, somewhere between the thudding of her angry heart and her gnarled clot of overwrought intestines, she feels greater rage rising, luminous bile ascending like venom to fill the fangs in the back of her throat. Her jaw burns. She swallows the scrapings of cake like a shipwreck victim sucking on lead.

Speaking through the fangs and the sensation of fire, keeping it all under control because she really can't blame him, because he's lucky and blessed just as much as she's been cursed, and neither of them chose to be born the way they are. Nobody gets to choose their parents. Synthia says, "It's hard for someone like you to understand. You're so athletic. Everyone likes you."

"Is that what you think? Yeah, I mean, it's easy to make people like you if that's what you want. Usually, it's like, you just make sure they never get to know you too well. Keep things fun. I wish people would take me more seriously sometimes, like they do with your painting. I go through that gallery hall on my way to Chem twice a week, and your figure drawings are wild. I was really impressed. Kind of frightening. I promise, I mean that in a good way."

Hand over his heart, his smile is way too admiring and kind, stoking the embers of her ire. Is he making a joke? He asks, "What's it like to have talent like that? Did you always know it? I think it must be amazing."

Not exactly slamming her fork down, but decisive. "People have been making fun of me my whole life."

"People are stupid, then. You've got to learn to ignore them."

The brown pile of shit-cake has stripped Synthia of her charm. Coagulating inside of her, it impregnates every cell with disgust. The fire of her silence screams like a siren.

Run, spider, run.

Did it dart away when she confronted it? Did her mother ever come home that night? What if the void of empty memory holds the secret to everything Synthia wants, and the spider is the guide who can get her there?

Then she must not be full, at all costs, or she'll never go through the looking glass. Or get back, if she's already gone through, as she sometimes suspects. She stands as demurely as she can with all the chaos and cake spinning inside. "I'm sorry. Excuse me again."

Something in him wakes up. Surprised, concern darkens his eyes. "I'm not making fun of you. I mean that. I shouldn't have given you a hard time about the cake. You're super talented and that's so much more interesting to me than getting trophies or cheerleading or whatever."

"Okay. I still have to go for a second."

"Don't be mad."

She lies. "I'm not."

The hurricane of rage blinds her, though she keeps it contained. Does she want this attractive and clueless man as much as she'd planned? Is he sincere, or is he playing another game, a big tease to make her believe and trust him so he can win whatever juvenile competition this is and then laugh at her behind her back with his friends?

She can't really see as she twists through the tables. The dining room has grown longer since she last passed through, making the journey more harrowing, the path less clear. Synthia's senses are on high alert, overstimulated by the paranoid siren of her disordered thoughts. Unable to parse her reception among the audience of diners, she's lost on the waves of judgment, critique, curiosity, and lust. The smallest glance from a stranger strikes with brutal impact. If only she could become weightless and float.

The loud group of young professionals has multiplied, taking up three tables now, shoved together at difficult angles that block her way. She changes direction. Forced into a crevice behind the creepy middle-aged couple who have finished their second bottle of Valpolicella and moved on to arguing over coffee, she squeezes past. The man's voice is cruel and low. There's no way by without touching his chair. Her hip brushes against his jacket. Synthia tries to apologize as his wife scoffs and says, "Slut."

Layers of conversation and barking laughter clattering through the high-ceilinged dining room seem to echo the word, as if more diners have joined in to chant "Slut, slut, slut." As Synthia spirals one way and then another, trapped in the maze of tables, her dress shreds against the baroque edges of the carved wood furniture and snags on the tines of forks raised by pounding fists. She's stripped. But no, it's only one small tear, just above the knee, so small no one can see it, but it's enough to make her blush.

Red, her face is red, she feels the moist heat of shame unmasking her face and painting it red. Not porcelain, not clean, not ever; little red riding hood running through a whole forest of wolves, barking and leering as she ungracefully stumbles. She's been lost here forever, starving, stewing, entangled with the hairy limbs of salivating beasts. They toy with her, a scantily cloaked piece of raw meat, a doll with red skin gone wrong, and the shit cake still inside of her, bubbling, metabolizing, copulating, filling her cells with fat.

A curtain, finally, a curtain hiding an exit. Behind it, she follows the arrow-shaped signs that say "Restroom" through a series of hallways with various doors, storage, past back entrances to other businesses, the halls silent. Empty. She's been away from her date too long. It's getting late—finally, a ladder. The arrow points up. She climbs to the door at the top.

She rushes to the first stall, not checking, not locking it, bile hotly rising like luminous venom from the fangs in her throat. The tubes and sacs inside of Synthia clench with practiced revulsion. But before she heaves, a voice.

"I know it's not really your birthday."

Synthia chokes and swallows, frozen in place.

The tap of lips pulling on a cigarette, an exhalation, and then, "I don't care, don't worry. Anyone can see it's that chud you're with. Want one?"

"I don't smoke."

Soft laugh, doors swinging, and the dark-haired server is in Synthia's stall. She's taller, broad-boned, with black hair pulled back in a severe ponytail and red lipstick that matches her pants. "Sure you do. Or you will. I know the type. I know myself. We're born to it. No way out."

If Synthia's heart races, the blood doesn't reach her feet to help her flee. The larger woman's outbreath envelopes them in a shared haze, smoke curling around extremities. Up close, the pucker between buttons of the black shirt reveals a red bra underneath. Synthia's curious if the server wears red panties to match, or black for a motley effect. Warming in proximity, a bitter rose fragrance emanates from the woman's skin. She's wearing black leather gloves, highlighting the white flash of her cigarette.

"Did you say your name was Diane?"

"Diamond," the woman says. "Diamond Snake. Yep. And before you give me shit about it, blame my dad. He was lead guitar in Tourniquet Tank, had his name legally changed. Diamond was my mom's stoned-ass contribution."

"Wow. I guess, well, you could do the same, if you don't like it."

"I've suffered this long. It's my inheritance. Here, shotgun the last drag."

Diamond sucks the stub down to the filter, holds her breath, and leans down toward Synthia's mouth. Confused, startled, with nowhere to back up, and Diamond's long arms spread out, black gloves pressed on either side of the stall, she shouldn't, she can't, she didn't come here for this, it's getting late, and she's been away too long, but the woman is commanding and regal. The woman is waiting.

Without releasing her breath, Diamond says, "Open up."

She does. Diamond blows downward from mere millimeters away. Synthia coughs, overcome with nausea and dizziness that wells from within like the humming of a swarm. She feels scattered into static, a fuzzy image of her former self; swirls, coughs again. Diamond catches her mid-turn, cigarette discarded, black gloves steadying Synthia, supporting her slight weight. Diamond settles below her onto the commode.

It's already happened. It's happening again. Luminous bile rising, but no, she can't erupt, not now, not on this woman, this beautiful woman who gazes up waiting, a light in her eyes like the bleached tears of a marble icon, oh no.

Synthia struggles without strength. A black gloved hand reaches up and holds her neck. The other clasps her side with long fingers that seem to wrap all the way around her waist. Diamond tilts her chin up toward Synthia. She parts her deep red lips, closes her eyes, and says, "Feed me like a baby bird."

Everything tight and trapped inside comes loose. Synthia drops onto Diamond's lap, pressing her mouth on the red lips, retching, shattering, unraveling from inside out. Hardly a trace of half-digested cake, but more, so much more comes out. Curses stored within her cells, the lust of one thousand hungry nights, filth tolerated for over two decades, envy that binds every gesture, and all the insults from birth to toilet training to puberty that have engorged Synthia's soul. She feeds them to Diamond, who strokes Synthia's throat, fondling with her buttery leathered fingers, encouraging, milking, probing for more.

Swallowing all Synthia can give, a history of sins, the history before she was born, the torrent of undesirable lives handed down and down again like frogs hopping out of her mouth. Emptiness uncoils within—the nothingness she's always wanted. A turning worm undoing all her knotted tubes, tunneling through to hollow her out in blissful cleanliness, all Synthia's wretched impurities exit the scene as if she had never been. But doubt as she thins and rolls and stretches, is she the tunnel or the worm? Where does Diamond begin and Synthia end? What is this something, this thingness within the nothingness? The ecstatic void calls forth liquid answers. Diamond sinks to the floor between Synthia's legs and turns her tongue upward to imbibe.

Swollen where the snake slakes her thirst, Synthia bursts with what must be the forgotten light of dead stars, glimmers in a black vacuum prickling behind her eyes. Her arms now press the sides of the stall as she braces her exploding center against the unknown.

"That's it," Diamond says. "That's good. Good girl. Feed me."

Synthia has now expanded to encompass a vast universe, yet she is honed to one precise point of pleasure like the tiny carcass of a mite, pinned in place. But pleasure is too simple an idea. She is opening doors within herself. She is becoming a new organism. She is an unexpected, unpredictable occurrence. Synthia has stepped outside of the repetitive, never-ending cycle of punishment and reward.

Synthia wants to eat.

Looking down at the black spider the size of a man's fist, mesmerized and terrified and feeling similar arousals she had no words for at this former young age, only the language of sensation, the mystery of erotic response as she touches her body, prodding and caressing her hidden parts to cease eternal slumber, to awaken and sing with the indifferent and honest voice of all matter, masturbating as a child, watching the spider as it watches her, its hunger transmitted on some psychic wavelength, or perhaps understood through genetically embedded signals recognized by the mammalian unconscious, programmed to know that what is smaller is prey. Yet the spider inverts this truth, mighty in its diminutive size. Fangs prickle in the back of Synthia's throat. Poison bile like venomous saliva tingles in each side of her jaw, the burn so reassuring.

Her mother's never coming home. The blinds are drawn but the back door is open, screen latched to let in a tepid breeze. Summer is hot, and Synthia's not allowed to turn on the air. "Don't you dare touch it," her mother says, the same thing she says about pee-pees, porcelain figurines, liquor, fancy bottles of fragrance, leftovers saved for the next night, hair perfected for a photograph, matches, fire, the flame of a candle, statues in church, the tempting vein that throbs in an excited woman's neck, and on and on, until everything Synthia should not touch must be destroyed, most especially what she loves. Because pleasure is and always will be inaccessible to her as a creature bound to contain her curse, bound by generations, unbound and unraveling now as Diamond resurrects her dead clit. She's either going to tear off the untouchable skin of the hard nub pulsing between fingers and teeth in self-castrating epiphany, or she's going to eat everything in sight.

The screen door swings open. She pounces on the floor and gobbles up the spider. Her mother screams. Grocery bags drop, cans roll across linoleum. Black legs crunch as she gulps down meaty, bitter liquid. Black gloves twitch as she shoots venom into her first victim.

Diamond catches the flash of light, of fang, a knife gleaming in the sun. One version of her survives while another goes missing, another gets fired later tonight, and another is found broken and bitten, her body drained of blood, wedged between the white toilet and black tiled bathroom wall. Every breath from Synthia's upper or lower mouth is Diamond's next last chance, a life inhaled and exhaled, a film they've played too many times.

Spider and snake entwined, clutched in passion's death-grip. Emptiness so full, end to end inviolate, that the body, this body, Synthia's body, refuses interpretation as anything other than the dark space between celestial objects. "If anyone asks me what happened here," she says as they break apart, "I'll deny that you exist."

Diamond sighs.

Synthia backs out of the stall, trembling, reciting words like a badly memorized script. "What do you remember? What did you see? Woman is a witness, the man is oblivious. Eating is the first sin. Eve and Adam were born immortal. Food is what introduced death into the world."

"So what do you propose as the antidote?"

To the sink, rushing, scrubbing, rinsing off any trace. There should be a soundtrack to orchestrate her actions instead of this glittering silence. "An eyewitness is useless. The way you can only see the weapon pointed at you in a crisis. There could be anyone behind it." Drying hands on paper sheets. "I'm late. I have to go."

"Running back to that chud? Sure, he's pretty, but there's no way you'll ever love him. Look at what you've done."

Synthia looks.

Empty of rage, she shakes her head and turns away from the awful sight with perfect poise. "No. You don't get it. I'm going to marry that chud."

She wants Diamond to laugh and then realizes things have gone too far for that.

With unexpected calm, Synthia risks the mirror to check her hair, her face, but she can only see Diamond behind her in the open stall. No matter how she twists and turns, the mirror has changed and refuses to cooperate. What Synthia used to see is gone, replaced by what she's done.

"It's okay. People go missing all the time," she says to her absent reflection. "That's why everyone likes true crime and murder mysteries, because we can pretend to get answers, but no one really knows the real story. Every confession is a lie. The real crimes are beyond murder, beyond reason. Sin is invisible. People vanish, and no one knows why. The bodies are never found. I am the bread of life."

She turns, it's late, the boy's waiting.

The door she entered says "No Exit," and the opposite says "Exit." Synthia makes her choice, which seems simple and obvious until she considers the consequences. So much depends upon which side of the looking glass you started from and where you lost count in all those crossings. It's hard for Synthia. Now that she's remembered eating the spider, she's even less sure of where she started, of how many mirrors have transported her, of how many mirrors lied.

Expecting to trigger an alarm, she shoves the heavy steel bar. She waits for the sirens. She'll be waiting for the rest of her life. One day, she might realize it's not that the sirens didn't go off; she just can't hear them until they stop. Outside in the dimming light and cool air, she is atop a brick staircase that wraps around the building and leads down through an alley to the plaza where pedestrians stroll.

Night is falling. Her date is waiting below, one hand in his pocket, the other carelessly toying with his car keys. He speaks to an older man in passing, their shoulders nearly touching for an instant, and then, just as quickly, breaking apart. She wonders how he knew to meet her all the way back here in such an odd alleyway, realizes Diamond must have sent him, Diamond must have survived, and hurries down the flight of stairs in a flurry of skirts and hair and clattering heels, full of her new-found emptiness, her new-found void. She feels certain about the boy, a perfect alibi for her life.

Nothing Here
Max Restaino

Delicate strands of cobweb wave from the ceiling. The smell of sweat rises off the dirty clothes which carpet the floor. Over my bed, the ivory sand swirl sky ripples like water, and through the clouds and cobwebs, I can see the skeleton's reflection: cloaked in tight skin, a glass eye like a lens in a forehead ringed with angry scar tissue.

The pinpoint of headache behind my left eye throbs like a rotten tooth, radiating through my scalp. I cover my eyes with my palms and focus on the distant horizon behind my eyelids—a thin grey line blooms, separating the lightless sky from the ocean. Arcs of electricity cross the mountaintops—spots of light glowing through gristle.

A stone protrusion thrums with my pulse. I envision it becoming gravel, then sand that remains trapped and rolls in irritated folds before blooming a pearlescent orb in the hills. Cracked white enamel browning, then black. Ribbons of infection blow through my hair like stale wind.

‡

I bring my notebook to work and draw boxes to pass the hours. Mind-numbing classic rock standards dribble out of the speakers, crawl across the ceiling, and rain on me like dust. Hours pass with no customers. People ask me how the store stays in business. I shrug because I don't know.

The front door is flanked by two small palm trees in fiberboard planters painted to resemble real wood. Kneeling beside them, I reach into their bulk with a pair of green safety scissors and clip off the dead leaves. I ask the plants if the music is killing them, too, but neither says anything. I try to read but the ringing in my ear is too loud to concentrate. The sun sets, awakening the sharp throb behind my eye. I seek relief in pressure points but find none.

Headlights fly into the parking lot as a minivan backs into a space in front of the store. The workman gets out, hobbles on a cane toward the door, and goes in. I hear him banging around on the other side of the wall.

Sitting behind the desk, I run my hands over the hard edges. Plastic-laminated particle board sheets with a wood paneling-dyed vinyl veneer line every side of every slab. In some corners the edge banding has flaked away, exposing the cheap wood underneath. I imagine breaking my nose on a stiff corner, releasing the pressure through a fissure in my face.

‡

The man from next door hobbles over to my store, swings the door open, and storms in, waving his cane. He asks my name, and I lie.

I built this building thirty years ago, he says. Now my uncle has me cleaning out that shit next door. Were you here when that guy was in there?

Yeah, for a while.

Real piece of shit, that guy.

He talks for a while longer. I pretend to listen,

and he leaves. Ten minutes later, he comes back with a power drill and rechargeable battery. The headache beats behind my eye, turning my stomach sour.

I built this place but I can't remember where any of the fuckin' outlets are. Can you plug this in for me? He hands me the drill and battery.

Sure, I say. No problem.

He comes back later an hour later

That thing still charging?

Yeah, I say, not knowing if it is or isn't.

I gotta run around the corner for a little bit. You're here 'til 8, right?

Yes, I lie.

I'll be back by 7:30, he says, limping to his van and driving away. I vacuum, water the plants, count down the register. At 7:00, I leave and take the drill with me.

The heavy tool's handle is made of smooth red plastic. Its rotating eye stares and spins, a black, sinister bit set in the center. Back at home, I put the drill in my closet then shove a pile of dirty clothes in front of the door. I take the last two Tylenol in the bottle and lie on my bed until the headache goes away.

I check my phone, send a text message that will go unanswered, run my fingers over the cracks in the glass, and fall asleep reading an article on the history of trepanation.

I toe the edge of a vast chasm. The sky casts crimson over the endless cliffside, a crescent of cement-smooth plateau. The darkness over the edge swallows everything. Cloaked figures gather, their eyes large orbs in pallid scar tissue, all lenses turned on me. An iron-tinged breeze blows across the gargantuan emptiness. I approach the figures, but they do not move. Shadows in swirling mist, cataracts shining like cat's eyes, recording me on the celluloid threaded across their bones.

‡

I spend my day off lying in bed. The ceiling is meshed and swollen with electric light. Words I can't read paint lines like slats of shadow. The same shapes repeat over and over. Rain pelts the roof and window. If I turn my eyes back and stare through the glass set over my bed, I see the world upside down, crystal rivulets trickling into the sky. My headache comes and goes, but like everything else, it feels far away.

Static electricity lifts me out of myself and into the glowing white. Alabaster light fills my eyes, broken by lines that intersect and expand into boxes that build a clean white tile room. The woman in the corner wears a white robe. She stands beside an open door, arm extended into the fresh air, cigarette burning between two fingers. Several men stand in the center of the room. One of them points at the camera, then at the gaffer tape X on the floor. I can almost hear what the man is saying, but it's far away.

A man wearing a black knit hat holds a machete in his hands. He calls over his shoulder, and the woman looks towards them. She tosses her cigarette into the dirt then walks over. The man hands her the machete, which looks larger in her delicate hand. She turns it over, then looks at the man with a question in her eyes. Words through cotton. The woman points to a moving notch in the blade. It depresses beneath her finger and reveals a U-shaped empty space in the fake steel.

There are more words. The pointing man does some more pointing. He waves the woman over so that she stands behind the camera. The man in the hat goes and stands on the X. The pointing man taps on the camera's glowing rectangle, and the woman leans in to look at it.

The world blows away like fog and I am left staring at cobwebs on the ceiling, headache blooming.

☦

The actress walked home from the studio, smoking another cigarette. This one was making her sick, so she tossed it into the gutter after only a few drags. She had been there all day and just wanted to shower, take a Xanax, and fall asleep.

The filmmaker was a friend of the actress's boyfriend, the writer. They were making a short film that she didn't understand. The writer told her that it was a comment on *quote/unquote Art Horror* while also using exploitation-era special effects. She wanted to ask him what the comment was but didn't.

To the filmmaker, the success of the film was hinged upon the fact that nobody would recognize the actress. Her identity as *nobody* would add verisimilitude, weight to the idea that viewers could be witnessing non-fiction.

The woman reached the concrete steps of her building and went inside. She climbed to her apartment, disappearing with each step.

☦

You are a crest woven upon the air.

☦

In sleep, I feel like different people—a soul split

into sections then sprinkled across a dozen different minds. Reflections of faces that aren't mine, even though I know them. In sleep, I go away. A worm sliding through pockets of earth, a temporary parasite. I am a ghost stuck within the halls of this body.

I dream of an axe that splits the top of my head. Blood erupts in a crimson mist, and my mind escapes with it. There are pieces that I'm supposed to remember, but they float off in the distance, hiding or just dead and rotting.

I go back to work and spend most of the day staring out the window at traffic passing on the highway or drawing boxes, stick frames to fill. Self-storage, or an "efficiency first" apartment building.

The stone behind my eye reaches grey tendrils into the nape of my neck. I wiggle in place to try and maneuver my spine into a more comfortable shape. Oil leaks off the wisps of dull pain and drips into my stomach, curdling its bile. Anxiety like sandpaper scrapes beneath my ribs. Mind-numbing music *still* dribbles out of holes in the ceiling. I turn off the radio and sit in the silent store, listening to the ringing in my ears, a high-pitched keening that shudders against itself in crackling bursts of feedback.

I used to take pills every day. Not for the headaches or the ringing in my ears, though I do wonder if they plastered themselves on my senses in ways I may not have realized; at least then, the boxes were easier to fill, even if it wasn't with anything worth sharing.

The sun sets later today than it did yesterday, and the sky is still bright when the workman speeds his van into the parking lot. I press my palm into my left eye. He hobbles over and comes into my store.

Hey, what happened the other night?

Sorry man, I've been really out of it. I forgot we closed at 7—

Is that drill here?

It should be...

I pretend to check beneath the desk and under the counters, in the back room, in the employees-only bathroom.

Shit man, I don't know. I wasn't here yesterday.

Yeah, me either.

Maybe the boss came in and did something with it?

He fuckin' would be the kind.

Do you want me to—

No, no, I got it, he says, then leaves, going into the store next door to do what work he can without his drill. From his van, he blasts the radio, music squeezing through the crack beneath my door.

‡

The actress stood in her bathroom, wrapped in a towel, breathing spirals into the steam that hung between the walls. She wiped a hand across the mirror and stared at herself.

She thought: *this is a face that no one will know, and that is the point of it.* In her bedroom, she opened the amber vial and poured two light blue ovals into her palm, popped them into her mouth, and swallowed them. The drawer on her nightstand was half open. She took out a glass bowl and a grinder, packed the bowl, and took a hit. Another. One more, then put the bowl back in the drawer. She lit a cigarette while coughing but decided that she didn't want it and put it out.

The actress lay in bed, staring at the ceiling, letting the ribbons of smoke tie themselves to the antennae in her brain. She rose out of herself and stared down at the nobody in her bed. A cold husk. She was bloodless. *That's why they have to use special effects.*

She fell asleep as a fog nestled against the ceiling.

‡

Here is where the air flows through my body—a delicate reticulation. There are no stones in my head. Scaffolding of empty stick boxes stacked to keep the sky from falling. She is here with me. Her body is soft silver smoke.

Is it you? Could you tell me if it was?

Beneath my fingertips, she blows away, and I sink out of the electricity hiding in the sky and into the sour sweat smell of my bed.

I still wait for you to respond to my messages. I know someday that *delivered* will stop appearing under the tower of word bubbles. At work, I draw more boxes. I'm starting to see you in them.

In dreams, I watch you dive over the ledge. The glass-faced men show me every angle. If there is a bottom to that emptiness, then I hope someday to find my way down with you. For now, her face is yours, and I don't think she knows. I can't even be sure myself, but what do I have to do except water plants and wonder?

‡

The actress stood in the middle of a lightless concrete nowhere. Slow red lightning cracked the sky before fading back to empty. Cold from the ground radiated through her feet, sharp in her calves, running dead tendrils across her thighs.

Her robe unraveled, ivory string tied around her waist, lured on. She heard the smooth ground scrape beneath the dry skin on her heels, the taste of salt and iron on a tepid breeze. Ahead of her was a shining patch of ground. The actress and her reflection stared at each other for a long time. There were so many faces she didn't know in the woman she saw within the trembling ground.

☦

I leave early for work so I can drive past your dad's house. Your car is still in the driveway—I think your brother drives it now. Sometimes, I see it on the road and forget it isn't you. Your dad's truck is gone, so I get out of my car and approach yours. The floor of the backseat used to be full of your clothes. Now it's full of garbage from fast food you would never have eaten. I glance at the house to search the windows for faces, but there are never any there.

At work, I pull up a blank white square and enlarge it until it fills the computer screen. The glowing mesh of woven electricity glows into my eyes, filling my vision. I search for the hiding horizon—opposite of the shore behind my eyes. The electric chime connected to the front door explodes out of its speaker behind me, and I fall out of the lights.

The Boss walks in with the Workman on his heels.

You don't know what happened to his drill, he asks me without stopping or even looking in my direction. The Boss is a short man who drives a big car and tries to fill any available space with his presence.

I say, I don't, but they're already in the back room, pulling up the security footage. I stand in the doorway and watch the message pop up several times as they get more frustrated. No Source Connected.

The Boss yells over his shoulder, how long has this been down for?

I don't know. I haven't touched it.

You guys have to tell me when things break. How am I supposed to fix them if I don't know they're not working?

I've never heard him say my name. I don't think he knows it.

The rock behind my eye throbs.

‡

I watch their rehearsal from the lights. Not that there's much for the actress to rehearse—its everyone else who have to work on their part, trying to make her fake death look real. She doesn't know why she has to be there for this. They can figure out gore without her. The writer is somewhere else, and she wonders where.

I try to send down waves of something from the lights so that she can feel my warmth on her shoulders, but I'm not sure if it works, so I get embarrassed and stop, withdrawing into the lights and falling out of the air above my bed.

The actress doesn't remind me of you, but still… There's something that I don't have the words for right now. Maybe I won't later, either. We'll see.

‡

I'm sitting on the edge of my bed with the power drill in my lap. I don't remember taking it down. The window is dark, and both lamps in my bedroom are turned on. My shirt is sweat-soaked and cold, clinging to my shoulders.

I pick up the heavy plastic tool and pull the trigger.

It whirrs to life in my hand, bit boring at the air. The grinding machine sound fills my ears. When I close my eyes, I fall into its labyrinth of whirling pieces and electrical impulses—a thoughtless post-human brain humming in my hands. Black ichor rises from the space between floorboards, climbing to my knees—surface shuddering off the echo from a distant wave hiding in the vast night.

The walls of my room fall away. Lamps sinking and consumed. Fire in the sky that shatters the black distances. I see her shoulders rise above the cities and the mountains, rivulets of scarlet raining into the sea.

‡

The writer sat on a bench outside of the woman's apartment building. A streetlamp cast a cone of yellow light around him, and overhead, fat, clumsy moths smacked into the lamp's glass orb. Dozens of people flowed along the sidewalk in both directions—a mutant river that defended her front door from potentially benched foes. His eyes were fixed on the door, heads bobbing by in blurred silhouette.

The violet sky turned black, and light pollution hid the stars from any eyes eager to read them. Foot traffic thinned. The woman's bright red hair shined in the night light of his eyes. She went up the concrete steps to the glass door of her building. The writer's eyes stayed sitting on the bench. He watched his body go up the stairs behind her, press the boxcutter in the small of her back, and follow her inside.

I watch him make his mess in the sobbing girl's small apartment. We all fill a small box drawn earlier in this story and have been left to explore their labyrinthian expansions. It's unfortunate that theirs connected, and I can't help but feel responsible.

And I can't help. But it's probably my responsibility to watch him make his mess. Crimson and pearl and translucent rivulets of sweat that carve through thicker fluids. His arms ache. Empty eyes pore over something I can't see.

When her chest stops moving, he takes the rag out of her throat and tosses it aside. She cannot sob anymore, and now she's just the dead girl. He does what he can with the tools he can find in her kitchen. She spills out of herself, sharp and sour smells hissing out of wide-open spaces. Spreading black on the carpet, staking her forever claim, tendrils of blood weaving themselves into the fabric of the apartment itself.

No one can ever say that this apartment doesn't

now belong to the girl in the truest sense.

☦

The ceiling in the actress's living room was dark with early shadows. Amber slats of setting sun drifted from one side of the room to the other. Cushions flowering beneath her hips and shoulders, stuffed canvas hugging the actress under her own weight. When she breathed, threads blew over the tops of sand dunes that rose to kiss her ribs from the inside.

Faces hung in the space between her nose and the shuddering ceiling. She knew them and didn't. They rose in the static electricity echoing off her eyes until their camera lenses bloomed stains on the pale paint.

She absently chewed through the skin on her thumb. Wisps of sand trickled out of the opening into the cracks in the wood floor. Her hand hung over the ledge, and her eyes watched the swallowing lenses. From the next apartment, the waking whirr of a power tool spun its sound through the thin wall.

☦

I've dreamt of you carved in obsidian, throttling the grey sky, a storm over the great empty desert. Are you the same material set behind my eye? You swell and weigh me down and keep me out of the lights. The excavation equipment is on my bedside table.

‡

She pulled a kitchen knife across the inside of her forearm, opening a smile that spilled sand onto the counter. The actress put down the knife and leaned over, drawing boxes in the sand with the tip of her finger.

When did this happen? She asked the room, but it didn't respond. More cuts, more sand, a flat hand over the bristling surface, then more fingered boxes. The grit drifts beneath her feet, scraping between soft soles and linoleum. Small, smooth stones in the dunes that flowed out of her skin.

Behind her eyes, the actress dove inside of herself, investigating the cavities where organs had been replaced. What he'd taken, written, and left behind.

‡

My headache follows me into sleep, a rail spike through my forehead that pins me to the ground. Overhead, I watch the sky turn inside out. Waves of crimson smoke bloom slowly—blood in water.

The hole in my head dilates, hands clawing their way out, shadows climbing free, dripping in grey matter. Ribbons of slime stream from my nostrils, etching roadmaps in the dust, a spiderwebbed corona of broken glass glowing around my head. Faces from the lights melt in and out of one another, a ring of uncertain flesh roiling between my nose and the sky.

I feel the pressure in my head still, you trying to escape, trapped for whatever reason. I'll take the blame. I really will. You're a seed I planted; I can't be upset that your roots have taken hold so surely.

Alabaster arms fall from the firmament. Fists that smash my head open against the ground, spitting you out like a grape seed. I wake up vomiting bile, a knife of light in my eye, power drill aglow on my table.

‡

She wasn't answering his calls or messages. The writer let himself in, closed the door behind him, and turned gut-first into the actress's kitchen knife. Stuck in his sternum, she forced the blade downwards, through his abdomen. It split like raw steak. Crystalline saltwater spilled across the foyer carpet. The sharp stench of saline tightened his nostrils. The writer fell sputtering, face first in the wet rug.

The actress lay in bed, shivering, a dozen dry slices from wrist to shoulder, the rush of falling dust. Her phone buzzed again. She didn't want to look at it, see herself reflected or not in its surface. Half-hanging over the side of her bed, she drew boxes in the sand.

This is the one where I live, and this is the one where he lives. She trailed off. The room still had nothing to say. Outside, a train whistle wailed across the sky. From somewhere on the other side of the floor, a small tide crept towards her shore.

‡

Are you in there?

The machine is heavy in my hands. I press the drill bit into the inner corner of my left eyebrow and pull the trigger. From outside, I see grit teeth, smoke, wet red in a spray, and ribbon running into my closed eye.

A snapping sound. A drop in pressure. Beautiful light in my head. Your crystal eyes in mine. Hands in hands, tangled ribs, skin climbing over me, both of us buried on the beach.

Like Snowflakes Melting on Your Tongue

Xavier Garcia

I was already tipsy when I first walked in here and that was when I first walked in here but now I've been here a while and while I'm not drunk, I'm also more than just tipsy. When I first walked into this strip club, I wasn't looking for a lap dance or anything. I just wanted to go from tipsy to drunk and watch some naked girls dance but then she walked up to me and asked me if I wanted a private lap dance in the back and I actually didn't want that. I only wanted to drink and to watch but I said yes anyway because it felt like the mean thing to do and now my pants are halfway down my ass and my cock is in this stripper's mouth and she sucks it so good and her lips are so glossy and plump and yet all I can think about is that I actually prefer my girlfriend's lips to hers.

Not that this girl isn't cute. She is. She's exactly my type. I look down at her and her long black hair pooling down her shoulders and looking so dark and pretty against her face so pale; her green eyes looking right into my own. When we first started talking, she told me that her family was originally from Syria and so she's worked her hijab into a kind of string one-piece bikini to honour her heritage but as she slurps on my cock that feels like a weird way to honour your heritage but who am I to judge it looks nice on her cocaine thin body and I like that she cares about something I wish I had that and it also looks comfortable, she was able to get topless really easily because now the headscarf isn't covering her breasts, now she's wearing it as only a thong. She's got bottoms on but no top that reverse Donald Duck.

I tell myself that I'm enjoying the blowjob. I tell

myself that this is exactly what I need. I do my best to stay in the moment and enjoy this for what it is. I try to keep myself turned on and to keep myself hard. I try not to think of my girlfriend to keep myself hard, so I retreat into myself like I'm not me getting a blowjob, like I'm someone else watching someone else getting a blowjob, like I'm watching porn, like I'm watching the most interactive porn I've ever seen, except this isn't like usual porn, my dick isn't nearly as big as the big dicks on male porn stars so this porn kind of sucks and I try to stay hard and I try to tell myself this feels good and I try not to actively wish that I cared about anything as much as this stripper cares about honouring her heritage and maybe she notices me start to soften because she gets more into it and I appreciate how nice she's being but because of the enthusiasm of her movements her long black hair fully parts down the middle so I can see the back of her neck and for the first time I notice that at the nape of her neck jutting out of her flesh is a skinless little appendage wriggling red to the rhythm of her up and down bobbing.

Without meaning to, I push back away from her in the small, private space of the booth. My cock slipping out of her plump lips. She's tasted the lordflesh. I had no idea. She looks at me, shocked, completely confused. And I guess she sees something in my eyes because her hand shoots to the back of her neck and she looks at me kind of embarrassed. Her eyes big and embarrassed as she licks pre-cum off of her lips because she didn't ask for a condom and I didn't have one even if she had. And I don't want to make her feel bad so I tell her I forgot I had somewhere to be and that I have to go now. But I don't think the lie is very convincing because I was already tipsy when I first walked in here and that was when I first walked in here and now I'm slurring my words. She fixes her hair so it covers the back of her neck and I pay her the money that we had agreed on even though we had only just gotten started. I tuck my softening cock back into my jeans and thank her again and promise that I'll try that Syrian joint that she recommended and then I zip up my pants and leave the private area of the strip club. I collect my coat and my umbrella from coat check and head out the front doors, leaving the dark of the strip club for the dark of the rain.

I guess it's time to go home. But I don't want to go home. But I guess that it's time. Even still, I can still take my sweet time. I decide not to take the subway home and that I'll walk it instead. And I know that it's raining and I know that we've all been encouraged to stay out of the rain but the fresh air is doing me good and I have an umbrella, after all. The paper-thin strips of lordflesh here and there in the rain can't even touch me while I have an umbrella and the little flakes of skin are so delicately dappled with blood that they look almost pretty as they dot the pavement in pinpricks of watercolour red before being washed away by the rest of the rain.

It isn't long before the restaurant and coffee shop chains of downtown make way for Brazilian churrascarias and Mexican taco joints and shitty tenement apartment buildings and government housing and future-fucked condominiums and I like my Brazilian churrascarias and Mexican taco joints and I can't help but hope that these future-fucked condo owners don't bring with them the restaurant and coffee shop chains of downtown but also who gives a fuck if they do. And then it isn't long before I'm walking through the doors of my apartment and riding the elevator up to my unit and I'm taking out my keys to open the door and at least I'm back to being just tipsy.

I open the door and see my girlfriend in the hall by the little table against the wall. She's all made up. Her long black hair all done up in French braid pigtails that pool down her shoulders and her slutty black dress. Her cleavage looks incredible. Little gold crucifix snugged tightly in between her breasts. She turns to look at me as she takes off her earrings and she looks like she's probably high or at least drunk and it looks like we're both getting home at the same time.

"Where did you go?" I ask.

"To break things off with him," she says.

I look at her slutty black dress.

"Did you fuck him again today?" I ask.

"Yeah. One last time. To break things off with him," she says.

I walk to the little bar against the wall on the opposite side of the little table and make myself a gin and tonic. I was tipsy when I walked in here but now I want to be drunk. As I make my drink, I tell her about the stripper and the blowjob and I don't tell her how I never went there for a blowjob but just to drink and to watch and I don't tell her about how watching the stripper suck on my cock was like watching someone else getting sucked on and I don't tell her how I really tried not to think of her to stay hard because I want this to sound mean. But even though her big green eyes widen as I tell her the story, she doesn't for a second look mad.

"Was she prettier than me?" she asks.

"Yes," I say.

She smiles because she knows that I'm lying.

"This is all your fault," she says.

"How the fuck is this my fault?" I ask.

But I wish that I hadn't have asked that because then she goes on her usual rant about me being careless with her, about me being careless with everything, how I used to care about things, and now I don't seem to care about her and now I don't seem to care about anything.

"Well, I care that you sucked my friend's dick," I say. The words exploding out of me.

Her big green eyes widen at my anger and I'm so tired of hearing about how careless I am with her and how careless I am with everything and how I used to care about things and how I don't seem to care about her or care about anything and I'm so sick of hearing all of those things even if she is absolutely right.

"I care that you fucked him again even though you said you were breaking it off," I continue, following up with more anger.

But her big green eyes grow less wide because she can tell the last part was forced. She can tell that

I'm only pantomiming the anger. Because yes, I do care that she sucked my friend's dick and fucked him again even though she said she was breaking it off, but if I'm being honest, it's less any of those things and more the inconvenience of it all, the inconvenience of potentially having to break up with her over her cheating and the inconvenience of losing a friend and I know I should be more careful with her and more careful with everything but dig deep as I might I have a hard time caring about any of this at all.

I make myself another drink. And she goes to turn around for the bedroom and her eyes are no longer wide and I liked it when they looked big and wide and green and pretty, so I don't let her go, I force the fight to linger on and I try to pantomime the anger more realistically this time and I call her bitch and I call her a slut and I call her a slut and I call her a bitch and I can't think of any other words to call her because I don't really feel them and then she finally closes the door to our bedroom and her cleavage looks amazing and her eyes aren't wide but she's smiling a little.

"Make me a drink," she says. So, I make her one and we head out to the balcony.

We sit on the little wooden chairs against the

brick wall of the balcony, neither of us saying a word as the rain falls down over the railing and here and there, you can see the red needlepoint gleam of lordflesh flaking down alongside all of the rain.

I sip on my newly made drink and I don't know why, it isn't to be mean, but I tell her about the stripper and the skinless appendage on the nape of her neck and the fact that she had tasted the lordflesh.

"Did you touch it?" she asks.

"No," I say.

"Was it hot?" she asks.

"Yes," I say.

And that last part surprises me because I don't think that's a lie, even if it did scare me.

I realize as I say it that I'm also turned on having admitted this to her. Not turned on by thinking of the stripper or thinking of my girlfriend, but turned on by saying the words, by admitting to arousal instead of pantomiming a feeling or performing words I don't mean and then I can't believe that this relationship is over, the inconvenience of it, sure, but also how anti-climactic it feels, how much of a waste, and I wish that I had been more careful, I wish that I had cared, I wish that I had cared about anything as much as that stripper cared about honouring her heritage.

I get up out of my seat and walk over to the railing.

"Be careful," she says.

I ignore her.

I stand by the railing and the rain dapples my face and my shirt. And where did everything go wrong? But maybe that isn't the question. Maybe it's more about where I went wrong, and I don't know how to change because I don't know what right looks like and I don't know what right feels like but it would be so nice to be and to feel right without having to pantomime it and if this relationship is over then maybe I can learn to be right and I won't have to be wrong anymore. And then suddenly, my girlfriend is standing right beside me and holding the balcony railing as rain dapples her face and her exposed chest. And I don't know why I do it but I look up at the sky, all cloudy and angry and grey, and I open my mouth to taste the rain and my girlfriend does the same and thunder roils in the distance and then the rain tastes coppery for a second as a flake of lordflesh lands and melts on my tongue.

My girlfriend is the first to pull away. She crashes

back to her seat and she looks so scared and I sit back down in my own. And I didn't ask her to do this. I just wanted to feel right and I just wanted to feel because this relationship was always going to end. Those future-fucked condos were always going to be built and those future-fucked condo owners were always going to move in and then the neighbourhood would eventually grow too expensive to live in and then me and my girlfriend would eventually be fighting over money that neither of us has and then we'd break up over all of that fighting because this relationship was always going to get fucked in the future.

I meet her eyes and her mouth is open like she's panting. And in that slutty black dress, her chest is so very exposed and her cleavage looks so pretty and then even in the dim light coming through the dark clouds above us I can see that the skin on her chest is growing so red and then she can see that I see and she starts to scratch at it and she looks so scared and before I can say anything I wince fucking hard because my skin feels like its bubbling like someone is digging the flesh out of my chest with a million tiny push pins, the stab and scraping out of the live tissue in my chest done needlepoint by needlepoint, and it surgery burns so bad I almost pass out but I manage to rip my shirt off just in time to see my flesh powder slough off in a trickle of skin out of the new hole deep in my chest. Blood splashes across my foot and I look up to see a skinless rope of meat jutting out above my girlfriend's breasts and whipping around like an angry, flayed snake.

The pain subsides and we look into each other's eyes. We look at the new formations that the lordflesh we ingested carved into us. At the rope coming out of her chest and the hole in my own. She stands up to get a better look and I stand up to let her. She inches closer to me. Her new appendage whipping around in agitation, her little gold cross tinkling with the movement. I don't know what to say to her. And I don't have to say anything because she reaches out and rims the new hole in my chest with one of her fingers. The new hole in my chest must be shy because it recoils at her touch and puckers up tighter.

She puts her hand down to her side like she's sorry she hurt me but then the rope of flayed meat coming out of her chest seems to finally sense the hole in my own because it stops all of that whipping around and now the tip of it is rimming the end of my hole. And then she looks into my eyes like she's going in and I almost let her but then I remember that she sucked off my friend and she fucked him again today even though she said she was going to break it off with him and before I realize I'm doing it my hand shoots up and grabs the spongy ropey thing coming out of her chest and I squeeze down on it with all of my strength and her eyes grow all big and wide and green and pretty and she groans out in pain and almost falls down on her knees as the fleshy appendage fights to get free like some writhing eel out of water so I squeeze down all the harder because I want it to hurt and I know that it hurts because little drops of blood trickle out the end of it and my girlfriend's eyes are so big and so wide and so green and so pretty and she's groaning so loud and I want to rip it right out of her chest but what's the point, it was me who future-fucked this relationship because I don't know how to be right and I don't know how to care that I'm wrong.

I let go off the skinless whip coming out of her chest and she falls into my arms. For a second I see a smile on her face that I've not seen in years.

"I haven't seen you this angry in so long," she whispers.

I don't say anything back. I don't say anything as I feel the tip of her new appendage resume its search for the hole in my chest. I don't say anything as the blood-smeared tip of it starts rimming my hole again. But I wince when the tip pushes into the hole. The appendage just above her breasts is too big for the hole in my chest. It doesn't fit but she pushes in anyway. It's too much. She's stretching it out. It's stretched way too far. She's going to tear the hole in my chest. I grip her hips as it pushes inside me. Gripping her hips so hard that I know that it hurts her. Gripping her hips so hard that I'm almost ripping her slutty black dress. But she lets me grip her as she pushes deeper inside me.

Our chests now flat against one another. Tears in my eyes as she pants. The skinless red rope coming out of her chest pumping in and out of the hole in my own. It doesn't fit. I can feel the wall of the hole rip just a little. I can feel myself trying not to rip any further. But neither of us moves.

"This hole belongs to me," she says, breathless.

I nod.

"Say it," she says.

"This hole belongs to you," I say.

But I don't even know if I mean it. I don't even know if I mean anything. I don't even know how to mean. But I repeat the words every time she asks. I take comfort in the pantomime and the pain. I say whatever it is she wants me to say as thunder roils in the distance and lordflesh mixes in with all of that rain just over the rails of the balcony.

Split Dick David's First Post-Op Blowjob

Charlene Elsby

David didn't talk about it right away. I don't know. Maybe if I were in the same situation, I'd let someone get to know me first before I mentioned it. I'd say it's the type of thing you should be up front about, but I think if he actually was, some people might get scared off. It's the sort of thing you might run away from if that's all you knew about a person.

But David seemed so sweet. I'd never known that about him if I'd run off immediately, just from that one fact. And once he explained it, and then when he showed it to me, it all seemed so mean of everyone else, not to give him a chance. It's one small part of what a man is. Like, he's a whole person, not just a dick.

Not just a weird-looking dick.

He said that his ex did it to him. She was always afraid of him cheating on her, and one day, she just snapped and did it to him. I guess he was sleeping at the time, or she couldn't have snuck up on him. He'd definitely have tried to stop her if he was conscious. He said that she went psycho-bonkers and cut him and that she did it so he wouldn't cheat, even though he wouldn't have anyway. He'd never have cheated on her, and he didn't know why she thought he would. She was just psycho bonkers.

He said one time—one time—she found a button in the bed that she couldn't trace back to any shirts of either one of theirs. But they lived in an apartment building and shared the laundry machines with the neighbours. It could have come out of the dryer with the sheets or pillowcases. Ultimately, David didn't know exactly why she did it. That incident with the button was months before it happened, and he said he'd never cheated on her.

She didn't believe him.

I don't think this is the same thing at all. It's not that he lied about his dick. He just didn't say anything. If he were cheating on her, he'd have to lie, not just not say anything. Right?

Usually, when a guy gets his dick out, he tries to get it a little hard, so it looks bigger, but not like it's hard, like they're trying to make you think that's how big it is soft. But David didn't do that, and I'm a bit of a dick myself, so I asked him about it.

"The doctor gave me something," he said, in the driver's seat of a dark blue four-door 2007 Ford Taurus, his limp dick in his hand. And then he cried. He fucking cried. I didn't have the heart to ask him what it was, but when I looked it up, I found out there's something they give guys after penile surgery that's supposed to help.

Which is what I guess it was, what she did to him—penile surgery. They treated it like that's what it was, sewing, stitching, bandaging it up. The cut was deep enough. I pictured him, showing up at the ER, dick in his hand, trying to hold it together. One long cut from the base to the tip, far enough down sometimes to cut into the urethra. They put a catheter in it while the rest healed up, but there's no way to really do it without a lot of scar tissue.

And that was the problem. When he finally let it get hard again, that scar tissue wouldn't stretch like the rest of it. I'd seen dicks before with scar tissue. Sometimes when they circumcise them (is it a doctor that does it?), they really don't seem to give a fuck. Dicks that bend left and right and backwards or down. I've seen the hard white tissue, like getting superglue on your fingers, and then the skin doesn't stretch there anymore, but everything around it still does. Still, if you try too hard to make it bend, you might just tear the healthy skin away from hard stuff. And that's what we're afraid of now with David's dick.

That's why he hasn't let anyone near it in months, except when he showed me in the car. And even then, he didn't let me touch it.

David and I went out to dinner, and he got a little upset when they didn't have a baked potato like he wanted.

"I'm sorry, we're out," the server told him.

"Then fucking make some!" he said, pretty loudly too.

She left, and then I guessed she'd come back with whatever potatoes they did have. Probably mashed.

"It's a fucking restaurant," he said.

"Are you really upset about potatoes?" I asked him.

"They have fucking chefs back there, and I know they have potatoes, so just fucking… cook them!" he said.

But I know he was really actually worried about his dick. He'd stopped taking the medication, and we had plans for later. I was going to go down on him, to show him I didn't care about what it looked like. He must have been all kinds of worried. Like, what if it didn't work? What if it never came back from the dead? What if, however hard I tried not to, I made a face when he got it out? I was so glad he showed it to me in the car. But what if it was different… hard? What if the harder it got, the more monstrous it looked, so that I didn't really know what I was getting into, having only seen it sitting there, lifeless, on a light blue jean backdrop?

I'm sure that's why David was so cranky. After we paid the bills, we walked to David's car, silent. I got in the passenger side, and I was worried for a moment that maybe I shouldn't just assume he was giving me a ride. Like, yes, we'd been dating for a month and a half, and we came together, and we had plans, but from his attitude, I thought for a second that maybe I shouldn't make assumptions like that—that I could rely on him for anything.

"Are we still?"

"Yes," he said.

"OK."

He drove to his apartment, we walked up two stories, and through the textured white walls, I could feel all the people inside, living their lives with their regular dicks. I felt superior, like I'd have a special experience they'd never, and that at the end of it, I still wouldn't be the one with the fucked up dick.

Poor David.

I wished he didn't project his insecurity as anger.

I wished that at some point in between dinner and sticking his fingers in me on the sofa, he'd stopped to wash his hands.

I wished I knew where his ex was now. It didn't make sense she wouldn't be in jail after that. Why didn't he ever say what had happened to her? What charges she got? Why didn't his friends say? And why, when I looked her up online, did her photos make it look like she was just some woman, with no pictures of them together, no evidence they'd ever been together, no smoking gun post saying, "Aw shucks, I've been convicted of dick mutilation, and now I'm doing three months with a year's probation to follow and then subsequent every other day dick restrictions"?

WHY?

Who really did this to you, and why? Fucking why? And don't say she's just psycho bonkers. When David thought he'd fumbled around enough, he licked his fingers, then undid the fly on his jeans and pulled his dick out through the hole of his white cotton boxers. I was supposed to get on the floor and suck it, I guess?

"Let's go to bed," I whispered to him.

He followed me down the hallway, dick swinging in the wind. It sure seemed like he was still proud of it. I turned the light on as he lay down on the bed and spread his legs, making room for me to sneak up between them. I grabbed the hems of his pant legs and pulled them off, and then his boxers. I kneeled between his legs and bent down, touched my tongue to the bottom of his shaft, and then grabbed his balls. David stared at the ceiling.

My tongue danced on the underside of his dick, its good side, and for a second at a time, I put the whole flaccid thing in my mouth. It tasted like rust and sweat. I licked it harder and let my saliva really flow onto it, to dilute the flavour.

David's dick started to pink and swell. I could feel

the bloodflow. But it was still tentative. I thought of everything we'd done to get here, and I rubbed my index finger along his perineum. I felt the tissue under it harden, and I heard David groan. His dick made a quick jump, and I caught the tip of it in my mouth and sucked—hard.

"Oh god," David said.

"Oh god," he said again as I held onto his balls with my right hand and grabbed the shaft with my left, now that it was big enough to get hold of. I drooled into my hand and stroked David's dick, tight but frictionless.

"OH GOD," David screamed, because the tissues that healed a certain way on a limp dick started to tear as everything rearranged itself in response to stimulation. This dick did not jump like it was excited, it was like a fish on the bottom of a boat wondering when it might be allowed to breathe next. Death shudders. I felt it sputter in my mouth, trying to decide whether to respond and face the pain or give up and stay dead. I palpated my tongue in response, encouraging it along. My cunt was soaked.

"Stop it, oh god stop," David cried. His dick got real curved, and I adjusted my stroke. It wouldn't go down my throat, the angle too acute. I bumped it against my palette and thought of how I'd rather it be my cervix.

But if I let his dick go, David might escape. I had him hostage, too afraid to do anything that could ultimately hurt himself, and I wasn't giving up my leverage. I sucked harder and tightened my grip, rimming him with my other hand.

I looked up at David's face, his eyes dead. He stopped crying, speaking, making any sort of sound. He wanted it to end but had also come to recognize that there wasn't any way out but through. I knew that look, that way of being, and because I did, I didn't feel anything for him.

I felt it first, and then I tasted it, and then I spit blood and semen on his bed sheets. The red was bright and streaked thick through the cloudy base, like adding food colouring to a sugar glaze. David's dick retreated, absorbing blood and cum into its folds. David rolled onto his side away from me and hid his face in a pillow, suddenly a much smaller man.

Why'd you lie, David?

And what did you do to deserve this?

Endless Wound
Sam Richard

The black foam tip of the sharpie tickled as Sara pressed it against her sternum. A medical examiner file was spread out on the countertop in front of her, along with a red sharpie and Nathan's Windhand shirt she had just been wearing. She wished it still smelled like him.

The wounds in the photos were multi-colored, but she'd have to do as best as she could with what she had on hand. The placements were perfect from what she could tell, comparing the illustrative wounds scattered around her torso to the close-up photos and markings on the xeroxed, black-lined drawing of a human body.

The illustration held nine stab wounds. Now, so did Sara.

Her perfectionism begged that she go and get a more varied palette of colors, as to more accurately represent what she was seeing in the pictures, but she steadied herself. This work didn't need to be perfect. It just needed to be properly placed. Like all the great masterpieces, it wasn't for anyone else. Only her.

Upon filling in the final shading details on her artificial wounds, Sara made her way into the bathroom, file folder in hand, and compared her work to the pictures from a more objective point of view. A few were a little shoddy, maybe not quite the same shapes as the photos, but the longer she stared at them, the more she felt them in her flesh. They were now her wounds. A bizarre transference from Nathan to her.

He was coming out of a bar after an evening out with friends. A few too many bourbons and shitty beers, and he heard the call of home–of bed, of wife–echo in his ears. Their house wasn't far, but the Minneapolis winter was in full force. He opted to walk despite this, figuring it would take just as long to wait for a ride. At his wake, Sara laughed through tears that they had always joked that his stubbornness would one day get him killed.

Only a few blocks from home and a group approached him. There was suspicion that they'd had an argument at the bar, but no one knew for sure. Or if they did, no one would talk. No known words were exchanged, or at least none that any of the neighbors reported. Within a matter of seconds, Nathan was bleeding to death from his nine stab wounds. All torso. Four of them hitting major organs.

The knife was left in the final laceration, stuck between two ribs, as the men ran off into the snowswept darkness. Having taken his wallet, they were awarded thirty-two dollars cash for their actions. In the end, that's what Nathan's life was worth.

Sara pressed her index finger into the final wound between her ribs. Comfort enveloped her. She pressed harder until the tip of her finger went numb, and the spot between her bones screamed. Pulling her hand away, her fingertip was discolored from the sharpie ink. She imagined blood. Trickling out at first, then hemorrhaging. It poured into the freshly fallen snow, blooming at her feet.

For the first time in a week, the tears came without urgency, without despair. They came with the serenity of longing. They came with the haunt of what could have been. Walking up to the attic for the first time since before he died, she didn't fight it at all and simply let herself cry. Her tears a trail up the dusty steps and into her long-abandoned, makeshift art studio.

The walls and floor were emblazoned with multi-colored layers of splattered paint. The exposed red brick of the chimney was the one untouched place. A single rusty nail stuck out from the bricks. It was where she placed each piece once it was finished and fully dry. A temporary home before it made its way to a friend, small gallery, storage, or an awaiting client–though there hadn't ever been many of those.

A blank oversized canvas was propped against the nearest wall, and she pressed her body against it, staining the white cloth with smeared eyeliner and tears. Having lost everything, she asked herself how she could go on; how had she survived?

The fabric was abrasively comforting against her flesh. She wished she could climb into it and hang on someone's wall until the day they got sick of her and had her hauled off to an auction or–much more likely–a thrift store. It would be her final piece.

Herself. A grieving widow with haunted eyes and nothing left inside. Someone else might love her like that. Perhaps treasure her.

Pulling away from her fantasy, scarcely visible remnants of her artificial wounds dotted the once pristine canvas. The image stole her breath, and she ran to grab a brush and paint, hoping she had some that weren't too dried out to be usable. After finding the colors she needed, she mixed them with paint thinner. Luckily, they all popped back to life. She grabbed another blank from the dwindling supply in her small storage recess.

As best as she could, she painted the wounds onto herself, now seated above the crude Sharpie versions. Instead of just using black and red, she assembled a palate of colors corresponding with the dark wounds. Doing her best to get every detail that so clearly sat in her mind from staring at those photos for hours each night. Their shape, their relative depth, the dispassionate tone they evoked. The torn flesh on one, the abrupt, almost blunt ending on another. How one of them was almost circular, as though in the tussle, the blade had twisted inside of Nathan's stomach. The little bits of yellow fat or just barely noticeable ribs. Strands of muscle fiber along the inside edges of the wounds.

She focused on the images in her mind and as carefully as she could rendered them back onto her flesh. And when she was done, she again pressed her body against the textured cloth, careful to not smudge them in transfer.

Sara's tears still fell, leaving additional smeared streaks of black and water trails. And it didn't bother her. When she stepped away to look at the first art she'd done in over a year, for one fleeting moment since Nathan had died, everything was perfect again, before an icy hand gripped her spine as she studied the painting. Given the transfer of the wounds from her body to the canvas, they were mirrored. Newly found tears streamed down her face, but they were something new, something different. Not mourning.

She scrubbed them off her flesh with an old towel and paint thinner, trying again but mirrored on her flesh, like a print transfer. Again, she did her best to make them as precise and perfect as possible, staring deep into the photos despite the fact that their images were burned into her memory. Flipping the canvas, she pushed her body into it for a moment and then took a step back, staring at what she had created.

Now, the image aligned with his, but it was awful. She couldn't feel them. It brought her no comfort, only a sickening sensation in her guts. Fresh tears fell from her eyelids. Not of grief—or not exactly, but also definitely grief—but something more akin to a complex feeling of frustration, failure, *and* grief.

They were her wounds now, not his. She removed the bastard wounds, hastily repainting the real ones.

‡

Her phone rang in the living room, and Sara took a breath before heading downstairs. She answered with a hoarse voice and tears still on her cheeks. It was Jamie asking if she wanted to go out for a drink. Telling her there were still a few spots available at the Bat Annex show in a week. Encouraging her to put something in it, even if it was older work.

Sara washed the paint from her hands and arms in the bathroom sink as they spoke. Jamie's voice grew distant as she stared at her painted wounds in the medicine cabinet mirror. Their detail and depth wasn't apparent in her rush to get them back on in the correct places, but it was good to see them. Grabbing a worn shirt from the hamper and hastily putting it on, she decided that the wounds were going to stay, at least for now.

A drink sounded nice, but she couldn't stop thinking about the wounds. About *her* wounds. She was haunted by the second imprinted painting she had done. The horrible one. She needed to fix it. She needed to do it right.

Jamie was still talking. It sounded like gibberish. Sara interrupted, saying, "I'd love to do the show," before hanging up.

She pressed her finger deep into one of the spots. She didn't need to take off her shirt to know where they were. They burned through her skin and into her soul.

Pulling the shirt back off at the top of the stairs, she grabbed another fresh canvas and got to work. First mixing the paints just right before re-applying the wounds. Extra care was spent to get every minor detail right, though she no longer utilized the photos or diagram in the file, rather feeling them on the inside of her skin, and painting atop the sensation.

It moved her in an almost spiritual way, like Nathan was standing next to her, watching her paint. As he had done so many times before. Those little moments of pure intimacy, of sharing in the process of creation with each other. In allowing the other into interior, private worlds.

She longed to hold him, to be held by him. She longed to take the pain of his lonely and violent death and hold it for herself so he wouldn't have to carry the burden. As the rush of emotions and memories came, she painted. She painted his wounds with such perfection that they could be in a medical journal.

When she pushed herself against the canvas, careful to not smear or rub, what came off on the other side was dark and obscured, missing the highlights and details.

A pain worse than failure carried her to her bed, where she fell into a numb sleep as the remaining paint on her torso soaked into the sheets.

‡

The morning light lured her awake and she stood on shaky legs too quickly, almost falling over. She was quick enough to catch herself on the closet wall. Rubbing the sleep from her eyes, she stared at the woman looking back at her. She didn't think she'd visibly aged much since Nathan died, but she saw it in her eyes. They carried a weight that wasn't there before his death, before her new life alone.

Her eyes studied themselves for a minute before she glanced down at her wounds. Most had become multi-colored lines across her stomach, hip, and breasts, but a few were almost entirely missing– reduced to little more than a vague smudge.

It hurt. Not seeing them. Not having them. It was like a blade was pressing into her, slicing through the flesh and muscle, fat and nerves. Kissing her bones. It stole her breath. Heart racing, she ran upstairs, grabbing more paint, thinner, brushes, and water.

Remembering the previous night's mistake, she did her best to layer them backward. Highlights and details first, then atop those the broader strokes. Colors growing darker as each layer went. Her heart slowed, and breathing returned to normal as she painted each one with delicate care and love. When she was done, she went back down to the mirror in the bedroom and stared at her creation.

There wasn't much to see, really. Mostly black with some dark red, but she knew them well. Each and every perfect detail was there, hidden and waiting to be revealed.

Back in the attic, she grabbed another blank. The last one. Briefly, she wondered what she had planned for it the entire lifetime ago that she made it, but the thought passed through her mind quickly as she placed the blank against the wall, wanting to complete the transfer before the paint had dried too much.

Pressing her flesh against the canvas was like

hugging an old friend. Like hugging Nathan, and she forced herself to break from it, for fear that she might fall into the yawning white nothingness. For fear that she might want that. Stepping back, she looked upon her creation.

It was perfect.

Each wound placed exactly where it should be. The strange process of the transfer giving the images new life and reality. Like someone had stabbed a canvas and it bled. To death.

In the snow.

Alone.

Sara stared at her masterpiece. She imagined it defining her entire life as an artist. Whether or not she ever got famous enough to have people discuss and dissect her work didn't matter to her. She knew that for her, this was the piece she would likely never top–forever be competing against–and that was ok.

Eventually her stomach cried out with a sharp pain. She looked down, confused at what was happening, to discover that she had been pressing the back-end of the paintbrush onto one of her wounds. Not enough to break the skin, but long enough to leave a hot red spot just under the residual paint.

It was amazing. Like she was alive.

She stood for a while, pressing the sharp end of the same brush onto the nine wounds, holding it hard enough and for long enough that all eventually made her cry out in pain and ecstasy.

This was all she did for the rest of the day, until the spots grew to large swollen lumps, and she couldn't stay awake anymore. She collapsed into bed, brush in hand, shattered, yet whole.

Her dreams carried her to the snow, where she lay sprawled out on the sidewalk, watching the occasional car pass until her mouth and wounds stopped producing steam, and the world went silent and still.

‡

Sara awoke to desperate, throbbing pain throughout her torso. Like hot pokers boring themselves outward. Before her eyes were even open, she clumsily worked her hands under the sheets and pillows and herself in search of the brush. She found it by her neck, sprouting out from the base like a flower.

The wood was flaky and dry as she pressed it into her wounds one at a time, giving each a chance to extinguish its searing flame. When she was done, the burn was mostly gone, replaced by a comforting warmth.

Opening her eyes, she had a thought and immediately called Nathan's old friend, Kyle. Within the hour, she was standing on his porch.

He opened the door without a hello. "This isn't a great idea…"

She shoved a wadded-up ball of cash into his hands.

He sighed heavily and waved her in. "It's gonna take me a minute to find everything and set it all up. Have a seat." He gestured to a faded brown couch with large dips in the cushions. So she did. And she waited.

Eventually he returned, pushing a mid-sized tool chest on wheels. It was red and covered in stickers. He then brought in a chair and a small table from another room, wrapping them with plastic. Rubbing sleep from his eyes, he pulled a long glug from his coffee, and sat unmoving for a moment before saying, "Fuck. Let's get this over with," and patting the chair.

Sara took off her shirt and sat down. Nine swollen mounds appeared on her flesh. Each with a dark center of smeared paint and deep bruising. Kyle tried to object, but the look on Sara's face told him there was truly nothing he could do to convince her otherwise. Then she pulled a piece of paper from her pocket and unfolded it, leaving it on the table. Nathan.

On a slab. Cold and dead and unable to talk or move or laugh or buy a round or offer an ear or a hug or a quick-witted response. Breathless.

It was always real since the day he died. Kyle didn't live in a world of imagination; he lived in a world of material reality. But the photo made it more real than it had ever been. More real than he ever wanted it to be. Cold gnawed at his chest, slowly moving its way up to the back of his neck.

Not tears. Those would come later, alone and in the dead of night. No. Numbness. It wrapped him like a shroud. The doer in him came out. He needed to translate the image from *dead friend* to *anything else*.

He pulled out his power supply and machine, wiring everything with an efficiency he'd rarely known himself capable of. Without her saying a word, he understood the assignment, pulling just the right colors from his supply and just the right colors to blend to make the other colors. This was his art now. And he treated it with the highest level of divinity.

The needle dragged inside her swollen flesh, but Sara didn't make a sound, didn't move a muscle.

It only took about twenty-minutes per wound, though some were longer and others shorter. By the time they were done, his hands were feeling the effort. Getting older had robbed him of some of his grip strength. But he looked at his work with pride.

Sara shot up from the chair and ran to the bathroom, inspecting the wounds in the dirty mirror. They were perfect. There was peace. And clarity. And something else vibrating under the surface, but she wasn't sure what. For now, it was good. He bandaged her up in silence.

Throwing her shirt back on, she grabbed the picture of Nathan, thanked Kyle, and was out the door before he could respond. Once home, Sara headed up to her studio.

She stared at her painting and then down at her bare torso. Each wound was covered with Saniderm, the skin inflamed and bright red beneath the clear material. The longer she studied them for differences, the more she felt them in the places beneath her flesh. Deep within her cells. It was the same longing she'd felt so many times since he'd died. But now isolated to nine points in her body.

Reaching into her pocket, she pulled out the photo of Nathan. Until the tattoo, she hadn't looked at it in a while, knowing those wounds as well as her own neighborhood. She compared the three versions. Him, her, and the blending of the two via the painting. And while she was proud of them all, something wasn't right. The way she felt the pain in her flesh was still wrong. Like Kyle hadn't gotten every detail quite right, and she was now suffering for it.

She grabbed a paintbrush and started pressing it into the wounds.

Her skin screamed, blood trying to rush to the surface. The swell was so great it could only manage plasma, as clear fluid slowly filled the bandages, meeting the pink already within.

Peace came over her as she pressed the brush through her faux-wounds and into the real ones. The wounds she shared with Nathan. The wounds she held beneath the upper layers of her skin.

Working the point around and into them, she tore through the Saniderm, sending pink blood and plasma to the floor beneath her. She pressed deeper, and it was met by bright, fresh blood, releasing the sorrow she had held onto for far too long.

Her body screamed. She knew what it was like to be him. Alone. In the snow. At one with everything. Fading out into nothing. Cold. Silent.

Forever.

Gravity pulled her to the floor and she saw first red, then black as stars appeared in the absent horizon of nothingness. She pressed harder, and the stars rushed at her like static on an old tube television. Not quite pixels, but tiny rectangles of white that suggested other colors at the edges.

She lived in this state, in the pulsing pain in her torso, in the vibrant lights glittering in the nothingness. And every time it started to wane, she moved on to the next wound and pushed the tip of the brush in harder, deeper, until her flesh was swallowing it like nine hungry mouths.

Time stopped existing. There was little else. Her arm muscles went beyond fatigue to a new place of dull remembrance. Her balled fists hardened like stone around the metal tip near the end of the thin dowel.

Until it all went blank. Everything was gone. She was gone. Into the void, no longer conscious or capable of consciousness.

She was like that for an unknown stretch of time,

somewhere between ten-minutes and ten-years. Until a distant bell brought her back together, slowly. In incremental bits and pieces. First as registration of existence, then of self, and finally of body. Of battered, enflamed, bleeding, beyond stiff body. With fists she couldn't open, and eyes that scarcely saw more than fleeting, blurry images: a pool of red beneath her, upon a wooden floor. A painting near her head. A masterpiece. *Her* masterpiece.

The phone was ringing.

She struggled to move. Her body was carved from marble. It wouldn't budge. It just screamed at her until there were tears.

Tears were movement.

One cell at a time, she forced her head to turn, just slightly at first, but then about an inch from side to side, which grew into more movement, as muscles and tendons and joints creaked and popped and ground like gravel against rockbed.

The phone had stopped ringing long ago.

The fingers came next, one at a time. An agonizing uncoupling of the ball, her fist had become around the brush. Pinky first, then up the scale, until the only thing holding the brush in place was the flesh it had bored into.

Then, the other hand, partially beneath her, but necessary for any further movement, like the untangling of neglected Christmas tree lights or the solving of a sequential puzzle. That hand was number than pained. At least until the movements began. Hot blood rushed back into it. Beyond pins and needles, like lava coursing through her muscles and bones. A cold heat, something unnatural. She screamed as the pain fluttered up her wrist, to the joint, but all that came out was a dry wheeze.

Before long, her tears ran dry, and her voice returned, cracked and raw. Little by little, new agony by new agony, she reclaimed her body over the day and into the night and into day again until she could finally stand.

Limping to the kitchen, she chugged water until she threw it back up. The cold liquid was like scratching an itch with a razor, just the other side of pleasure. She opened the fridge, but the smell was off. Grabbing some boxes from a cabinet, she crashed onto a chair and started eating. First one box, then another, then another. She wasn't sure what she had. She just ate until the sensation of her stomach eating itself started to diminish.

Her bones ached and creaked, and there was a constant throb in her head and eyes. And jaw. And neck. And shoulders. And back. And hips. And arms. And chest. And all the way up and down.

But her torso hurt the most. Bulbous and engorged wounds wept sickly fluid and dull red-grey blood. Even approaching them with her hands was perfect agony. If only she could live like this.

When the food and water brought her to near humanity, she checked her messages: there were twelve. Most didn't matter, but several were from Jamie, asking first if she needed anything for the show. Then, rising panic and questions if she was alright as they went.

Sara had forgotten about the show. Limping to the living room, she turned on the television. It was Friday.

She spent the next several hours preparing: loading her car with the painting, her brush, getting her outfit picked out, doing her makeup, breathing through the pain. Taking long stretches to reflect on her life, on Nathan, on the nature of her wounds, on the nature of her work. She had to be perfect for the show.

When she was done, she reached down and touched the nine wounds. They cried out, but she circled her fingers over them. More strange fluid leaked out. It held a foul odor, but she didn't care. They truly were hers now.

Grabbing the folder from the kitchen table as she headed out the door, Sara said a silent prayer to Nathan, thanking him for the life they'd built together. Half cursing him for the life she'd had to endure alone.

Those thoughts followed her along her drive to the gallery. Inside, artists of all sorts were finalizing their art displays in a whirlwind of organized chaos. Three people were standing near a blank wall in the corner. One of them was Jamie. The other two didn't even register.

Jamie spotted her walking toward them and ran to hug her, "What the fuck!?" painted on her lips. They embraced, and Sara let out a whimper.

"Oh my god, are you ok?" Jamie stood in awe at her friend, jaw hanging open. "You look like shit..." She trailed off.

Sara pushed by her, managed to squeak out, "Is this mine?" to the pair who were standing there. They looked at each other and then at her and each other again, their expressions approximating pity, or disgust, or concern, but they didn't say anything. They simply moved out of her way.

She set her painting down against the wall, covered in a sheet. Jamie came over, "Seriously, are you ok? What the fuck, Sara?" But all Sara heard was the buzzing of bees.

Opening the folder, she stared at Nathan's wounds one last time. Despite Jamie's pleading, Sara simply stood. In front of the covered painting. In a random area of the front room of the small gallery. Surrounded by art and artists. Over a few dozen minutes, they finalized their pieces before the gallery head proposed a toast to all the artists.

Sara didn't move.

When they were done with their minor celebration, the doors were opened, and slowly, people began to pour in. Jamie kept grabbing at Sara's arm, trying to get her to leave. Trying to get her to answer. Trying to get her to respond at all. Trying to get her to even acknowledge her.

Shivers moved through Sara. Her bare feet and legs were cold. Her body screamed, and jolts of fresh pain permeated her every cell whenever Jamie tried to get her to pay attention.

Eventually, the buzzing stopped, and the thing pulling at her ceased.

Sara looked on, truly taking everything in. The

place was packed. Paintings covered the walls, and sculptures, both on stands and large enough to sit on the floor, were scattered about.

Onlookers kept walking by her with puzzled expressions. Once a large group passed, she knew it was the right time.

Without a word, Sara set the file on the floor facing out. Then she turned and pulled the sheet, revealing her painting. Nathan's nine perfect wounds on a pristine canvas. Staring at them, she sensed them in her flesh. This thing they shared that was deeper than death. Deeper than life. A unification of all things.

She pulled the brush from her pocket and then dropped her coat.

A few attendees stared at her naked back, confused. A few let out knowing chuckles as if to say, "Oh, it's gonna be one of *these* art shows…"

Sara didn't hear them. She pressed the end of the brush into a wound on her chest and shuddered, stars swimming in her vision. It wasn't agony.

It was silence.

Through the inflamed skin, the freshly grown scabbing, the pockets of infection. Past the fat, through the muscle, until it connected with bone. Foul blood met fresh. Yellowing pus, grey-pink blood, and fresh dark red all collected at her feet as Sara turned to meet her audience.

Gasps and screams echoed in the small room, but they were few and far between. Most just watched in horror. In awe. In both.

Removing the brush, she moved to the next wound over. Same game. Same result, though the smell grew worse, and bitter acridity filled the air. This one almost took her to her knees, but she fought the pull of gravity, letting her will overpower the glitching of her nervous system. The stars lasted longer this time.

As did the silence.

One by one, she pressed the brush in until it stopped, blood pouring from each wound like nine broken spigots and the red pool growing ever larger below her feet, glistening in the fresh white snow.

When she got to the final wound, the one that went between her ribs, the stars grew too great, and she floated to the ground. Her impact was gentle and warmer than she anticipated. Sara pressed the brush in deeper, giving as much of her waning strength as she could.

The stars flashed and shimmered, as snow fell around her. The lull of sleep called out her name over and over and over, and she let herself succumb to it, just like Nathan had.

Before the world went black, Sara watched smoke poured from their open wounds. Smoke which carried into the sky, blotting out the glimmering stars.

She was him, and he was her, and there was nothing separating them anymore. They shared in the everything.

Joe Koch writes literary horror and surrealist trash. Their books include *The Wingspan of Severed Hands*, *Convulsive*, *Invaginies*, and *The Couvade*, which received a 2019 Shirley Jackson Award nomination. His short works appear in *Nightmare Magazine*, *Southwest Review*, *Vastarien*, *The Mad Butterfly's Ball*, and many others.

Find Joe (he/they) at horrorsong.blog.

Max Restaino is an author from Poughkeepsie, NY. His first book, *COYOTE*, is available from Amphetamine Sulphate.

Xavier Garcia is a writer/editor from Toronto, Canada. His short fiction has appeared in various magazines and anthologies published by *Fugitives & Futurists*, *Cold Signal*, *hex*, *HAD*, *Apocalypse Confidential*, *Cursed Morsels*, Filthy Loot, and others. You can find him walking the nightmare corpse-city of R'lyeh, or at twitter.com/xavier_agarcia.

Charlene Elsby is a philosophy doctor whose books include *The Devil Thinks I'm Pretty*, *Violent Faculties*, and *The Organization is Here to Support You*. Her essays and interviews have appeared in *Bustle Books*, *The Millions*, and the *LA Review of Books*.

Sam Richard is the author of several books including *The Still Beating Heart of a Dead God* and the award-winning *To Wallow in Ash & Other Sorrows*. He has edited ten anthologies, including underground hits like *Profane Altars: Weird Sword & Sorcery* and *The New Flesh: A Literary Tribute to David Cronenberg*. His short fiction has appeared in over forty publications. Widowed in 2017, he slowly rots in Minneapolis where he runs Weirdpunk Books. You can stalk him @SammyTotep across socials or weirdpunkbooks.com

- ANXIETY VOL. 1
- DIRT IN THE SKY
- FUCKED UP STORIES TO READ IN THE DAYTIME
- FUCKED UP STORIES TO READ IN THE DAYTIME 2
- FUCKED UP STORIES TO READ IN THE DAYTIME 3
- FUCKED UP STORIES TO READ IN THE DAYTIME : THE BOOK
- ISOLATION IS SAFETY
- LAZERMALL!
- LITTLE BIRDS
- LITTLE BIRDS (GREEN)
- MICROPLASTIQUE VOL. 1
- PSYCHO NIGHTMARE FREAK-OUT
- SOFT CEREMONIES
- TEENAGE GRAVE
- TEENAGE GRAVE 2

www.ingramcontent.com/pod-product-compliance
Lightning Source LLC
LaVergne TN
LVHW092055060526
838201LV00047B/1402